RELUCTANT SUCCUBUS

and Other Tales of Sacrilege

by

TYTUS BERRY

2022

Hell is truth seen too late.

Thomas Hobbes

CONTENTS

Introduction

Reluctant Succubus
(a novella)
9

Phantom Limb
73

Sad Potatoes
94

The Definitive Act
102

For "Evan," "Clarence," "Angela" and so many others.

Introduction

If the "Reluctant Succubus" tale seems really lived in, that's because it was. And it's still very fresh in my consciousness.

There was a time in the early to mid-decade of the last millennium when the darkest music gave many of us the fiercest hope. The sense that real, important things were being communicated, and honest, terrifying things were being faced, and that, if enough of us really cared—if enough of us could endure the daily, hourly inanity and absurdity of what was laid out before us, and transcend our own nihilism, something might change. We might change.

The setting of this story is stark, but we laughed. We laughed and we drank and we caroused, and maybe because of the sheer enormity of the deeply-rooted, fucked-upped-ness that was encroaching upon us from every direction. Or perhaps we were simply indulging in the usual escapism. We found ourselves fearful, but curious and anxious, but fascinated.

We knew darkness. We encountered poetry. We experienced truth.

The other three stories in this collection spring from the same vein.

Tytus Berry
March 25, 2022

RELUCTANT SUCCUBUS

It's cool, it's hot
It's everything I'm not

"D'Bop"
Dirty Harry

Hello.

My name is Evan Phillips and I don't figure that much into this story, really.

Well, maybe more than I thought—on the tail-end of the tale so to speak.

The thing is, one of my best friends disappeared back in 1994 and we never knew why or how or what happened to him. And twenty years later I get a call from the Austin Police Department.

It's not absolutely relevant, but I'm a Black man, and my missing friend was a White guy. We were employed by the same market research firm off Great Hills Trail in North Austin back then, and we worked hard and played hard. We played really hard.

His name was Henry Nilson, but we called him Hal and everybody pronounced it like "howl." He and my friend Clarence, another young black man, shared one side of a duplex (two-bedroom, two bath) near the Arboretum and, at the time, I was living on their couch. Actually, Hal's couch, a black leather, three-piece sectional. It was the first piece of furniture he ever spent real money on. It was not a bad bed, and I guess you could say I broke it in.

The 90s were an excellent time to be young, living on somebody's couch and playing hard in Austin; but we weren't slackers. We were fine (if not refined) examples of that era's Sixth Street bar scene and perpetually unhinged capitol city debauchery. I've stopped telling some of the stories, because people today, especially young people, don't believe me. But this particular story, I have to tell. I wouldn't say I owe it to Hal—I would just say it's a story that needs to be told. People, again, won't believe me.

But I was there.

WE HIT THE SCENE on Sixth Street three to four times a week and still held down overpaying white collar jobs. It never took much to start off a night of boisterous, sometimes gradual and sometimes rapid-fire inebriation. If it wasn't me or Clarence working up a thirst, it was Hal. And it seems like it went on like that for a decade, but that may just be my liver talking. It was really just three or four years, and I remember that time fondly if not hazily.

I was younger than Clarence or Hal, and only Hal had finished college. I completed my degree in the years following our Sixth Street daze, but at the time, I was just having fun. We were all working at the same grind, but we each approached it differently. Clarence and Hal were managers with quarterly bonuses. I'd started before Hal, but left for another unsuccessful semester at college and then returned. Clarence treated the job more like a serious vocation, and sometimes even carried a briefcase. For Hal it was more like an airport layover before going on to something else. That occurred to me then, I think, but I realize it more now. But that's how I wound up on Hal's couch. He and Clarence had rented the duplex after I left for college, and then I was back.

Clarence and I were more like regular people, but Hal was a little different. For starters, the twelve-foot walls of the duplex—which was rented in Hal's name—were covered with personages from his pantheon of cultural influences. He copied their images onto transparencies, and then used an overhead projector he borrowed from work to blow them up on the walls. He traced the lines with pencil, and then painted directly onto the eggshell walls with black paint. So, depending on where you were standing in our place—where they let me stay for free—you sat or stood (or, in my case, slept) under or near the watchful gaze of the three- to four-foot-tall countenances of Albert Einstein, Frederick Nietzsche, Albert Camus, Malcolm X, Beethoven, Che Guevara, Gandhi, Van Gogh, Franz Kafka, etc. Most of our visitors couldn't even identify two or three. Hell, I only recognized three or four, and their faces followed us all over the duplex. As I previously noted, Hal was a little different, and only after he'd been missing for years did I fully realize that—again— for him, anyway, Austin had just been a stop-off before he moved on to bigger and better things.

I had been wrong, of course.

Austin was the end of everything for Hal. Austin was the last place he was ever seen.

"Head Like A Hole"
Nine Inch Nails

Hal was a trip.

He was up for anything with us, but he really wasn't one of us. Writing about him now makes me smile. Even after I've found out what really happened to him.

Perhaps I should preface that with explaining what I actually meant by "playing hard."

Hal almost always drove us down to Sixth Street from the duplex because he had an uncanny talent for operating motor vehicles while extremely intoxicated. This was before Uber. And at least two times we got pulled over when he was thirty-three sheets to the wind, and he never got nicked. He even challenged a pair of Austin's finest to give him a sobriety test once, and it caught them off guard. It was a startling (and, looking back), recklessly brazen example of reverse psychology. The patrol officers backed off, practically apologizing for pulling us over.

Hal had a distinctive Southern drawl, but his level of diction—his vocabulary—was huge, and he could get you back on your heels quick. Another anecdote that makes me laugh involved one of our God-bothering co-workers. This guy—Cory was his name, I think—he would half-playfully harass Hal toward the end of every week about accompanying him to church (the denomination of which I can't remember) the following Sunday. It was a long-running joke, but Hal was not some half-ass agnostic. He was an acknowledged atheist. He didn't believe in Heaven as an actual place or destination. He didn't believe in Hell as a destination for punishment, much less damnation. In fact, he said if he was wrong and God did exist, he had beef with Him. That God had a lot to answer for.

Cory badgered Hal for months and, then, one Friday, Cory caught Hal in a bad mood or struggling with a wicked hangover. I've never forgotten it. "I'll be there this Sunday with bells on, Cory," Hal said, ". . . if your pastor agrees to debate the existence of God with me in front the whole congregation."

Heads popped up above every cubicle within earshot.

Challenged—especially in front of the sudden audience—Cory vowed to inform his pastor, and said he would be happy to set it up. But Cory never mentioned church again. And Hal never went.

But it was more than that. A little while back I watched *The Great Debaters*, about the legendary Black 1935 national championship debate team from Wiley College in Marshall, Texas. I learned that for any debate, you had to prepare yourself to argue both sides of an issue. That's how Hal was. He knew arguments from both sides. He could defend most believers' beliefs better than the believers themselves. If that makes any sense.

But I digress.

We always started drinking at the duplex and then went somewhere for inexpensive spirits or to further enhance our spirits cheaply. The fact that none of us were cowboys or even remotely interested in country and western music (or dancing) notwithstanding, seventy-five-cent pitchers at Dance Across Texas was always a solid go-to. Hell—the fact that we were all roaring heterosexuals notwithstanding, we also hit Oil Can Harry's and any number of gay bars if they had good drink specials. We didn't discriminate where cheap libations were concerned, and—to be frank—it was usually more unpleasant to brush off a heterosexual female's request for a spin around the dance floor than a homosexual male's. The ladies sometimes took it personal, but the gay guys were always cool. You just had to tell them you were straight and they left you alone.

But that was another weird thing about Hal. He never asked anyone to dance. He just went out on the floor and started dancing. Sometimes girls would join him, and sometimes not. He didn't care either way, and sometimes he was the first one or the only one out there. It was like a Pagan ritual for him, and a form of self-expression. It was like "Howl" was howling at the moon. He was also a regular in slam dances and mosh pits. Some folks dug it, some folks didn't. Hal had fans, for sure, and some favorites. But the only girl I know he had a half-ass relationship with the whole time was this gorgeous Black girl who worked as an ad rep for an Austin radio station. Her name was Angela. She has her own advertising firm now. But, back then, well—for whatever reason—she and Hall were down for each other. And sometimes close. Never really together in a full-time dating relationship in the traditional sense, but still down for each other. I saw her at the duplex pretty regular, especially late and sometimes early, attempting to make a quiet, inconspicuous departure. What can I say? You learn a lot when a living room is your bedroom.

Most of mine and Clarence's Black friends that came around the duplex and saw Angela with Hal were surprised and didn't get it. They thought Angela was "legit" and didn't understand why she was hanging out with a White guy. Things were still a little different back then, even in Austin. And even for some Black people. But they didn't know Hal.

I'm not sure why Angela and Hal were never officially a thing, but I think the problem was she was friendly and light, and he was detached and heavy. Philosophically speaking, he could be melodramatic and sometimes even dark. Angela was climbing the ranks of the advertising world, and that required a big smile and sustained amicability. Hal was usually amicable and he could be a total blast, but he could also be morose and distant. I really think Austin was more like Hal's time in the wilderness, if you know what I mean. But it was also ironic. If I forgot to mention it, Clarence and I whiled away the off and after hours with White women, and Hal was involved with a Black woman. And I think he really liked her.

WE HAD OUR PRE-PARTY SPOTS and then our early evening spots, where we would often bump into some of our co-workers. Bars like Maggie Maes or Toulouse. Sometimes Touché for shots. Maybe a stroll through Steamboat, places like that. Tame Top 40, nothing edgy. Lots of sorority girls and fraternity boys and former sorority girls and former fraternity boys. Hal called them "civilians." We were usually buzzing by then, and scouting for prospects or being scouted. Clarence had a keen eye for mudsharks. The word "mudshark" is what people would describe today as a derogatory or offensive term. To me and Clarence—back then—it was a harmless, somewhat humorous (to us anyway) label, a playful gag. I don't know who came up with the word; it may even have been Clarence. But, generally speaking, it was a term we used to identify White women who preferred Black men. *Generally speaking*, because we kidded Hal about being a "mudshark," too.

Anyway, showtime was usually a club called Sanitarium back in the day (especially on Wednesday nights), or later, Acropolis. And I think there was another bar called Infinity, which played late New Wave, disco and rap—or what was then starting to be called "Gangsta rap" and HipHop. That was always fun. Especially when some of the brothers would be showing off their moves in a circle in the corner and Hal would jump in doing his crazy thing. It surprised brothers at first, but they got into him after a while. I wouldn't say Hal was a great dancer, but he was physically uninhibited on the dance floor and he didn't lack confidence. I think he'd even mentioned taking ballet for a physical education credit in college. Regardless, you could say he definitely danced to the beat of a "different drummer."

The other weird thing about Hal was his taste in alcohol. It didn't exist. He didn't like the taste of beer or liquor or enjoy cocktails or wine of any kind. *He just liked what they did to him.* He said he liked losing control. He said he just enjoyed "taking a breather" every once and a while. Hell, Hal didn't even drink coffee. The dude was a little crazy, but he was one of my best friends.

And then he just disappeared.

"Over the Shoulder"
Ministry

So, twenty years later, Austin PD Detective Sergeant so-and-so calls me out of the blue. I remember it clearly. It was a Wednesday and I was at work. I was a copy editor for the *Austin American-Statesman*. Over six hundred people had just been killed in clashes between protesters and police forces in Egypt, and one of them was a former UT student. It all happened after a *coup d'etat* staged by the Egyptian military, and now there was a local tie-in. So, we were really busy.

Detective so-and-so asks me if I knew Hal back in the day.

I say I did. I say he disappeared. "Did you find him?" I ask, suddenly distracted from our copy deadlines. "Have you found him?" Memories start washing back over me. I hadn't thought about Hal in a while.

"No," the detective says.

I ask him why he's asking. I ask him if something has happened.

"We'll get to that," the detective replies. "We'll get to that, I hope."

By then I'm married and have two kids and I'm smack-dab in the middle of an international conflict with local and national angles at the *Statesman*. Clarence is working overseas on some kind of oil exploration project. He's also married, but no kids. Detective so-and-so is having problems reaching Clarence, but he's able to locate me. He says it's about Hal and asks me to come by the station. He tells me they need some help on the case. He assures and reassures me I'm not a suspect.

I don't know what to think.

BUT I HAVE THIS WEIRD flashback.

Hal is out on a dance floor full of freaks jumping up and jerking around to a pounding techno beat sliced by psychedelic lasers. Suddenly the music and the lasers stop—and the contorting figures collapse on the dance floor, on their stomachs, backs and each other. They lie perfectly still for several long beats in the dark, until the music and the lasers—dialed down to lucent scribbles—start again, really low. The dancers remain frozen. They don't start moving again until the sounds are deafening and the lasers are a gamma brainwave. And then they're all spastic. Hal stands up and pulls this girl up with him, by her hand. They smile, spin, and bounce away.

"Hallucination Generation"
Gruesome Twosome

There I go, getting ahead of myself again.

So, showtime for me and Hal and Clarence was Sanitarium, Acropolis, Infinity, etc., depending on the year and the day of the week. But I forgot mention the after-hours bars. The after-2 a.m. bars, when alcohol was no longer served.

None of us were ever into the drug scene, ecstasy, LSD, Cocaine, whatever. I vaguely recall infrequent dalliances with "shrooms," but it was mostly just alcohol. Copious, way out and sometimes blackout amounts of alcohol. Times when no one remembered who drove home, how we got home, or whose house we were in if we didn't make it home. And, perhaps worse, whose bed we were waking up in. One time in '93, I wound up crashing at a big party house off Spicewood Springs Road. I woke up on the hardwood floor of a long hall across from Flea of the Red Hot Chili Peppers—and neither of us knew how we got there.

I think kids are smarter than that these days, or at least I hope so. I hope my kids will be.

Anyway, there weren't many after-hours bars, but sometimes they really came in handy. Sometimes you could dance a solid drunk off at an after-hours club, or at least rally your brain cells before the journey back up MOPAC or Capital of Texas Freeway. One of the after-hours bars was reggae, but, as none of us were serious about the *ganja*, we hardly ever went there. We loved Bob Marley, but we weren't stoners. Another might have been a jazz bistro, but jazz was definitely hard for me to enjoy unless I was in the right mood, and the right mood for us was not plastered out of our minds at 2 a.m. After-hour bar libations were usually limited to water, cranberry juice or orange juice and nonalcoholic pina coladas, ginger ale or soft drinks.

Hal's favorite after-hours bar was this place called Tomes, and I'm not sure Tomes even opened until 2 a.m. In fact, I'm pretty sure it didn't. Tomes didn't start up until almost everywhere else was shutting down. Tomes was for the harder cases, vampires, transvestites, freewheeling grannies, ecstasy-addled Club Kids, Dub Kids, Emos and the nocturnally bent of every type. Hal fit in, sort of. He didn't wear make-up or dress in black, have a tab of acid under his tongue or drain glasses of orange juice to extend the effects of ecstasy. He just wanted to keep dancing, keep moving, and keep going. He never wanted it to end. So, after all the other bars, we'd be at Tomes at 3 a.m., shit-hammered and bleary-eyed, but stark-raving invincible.

AS I RECALL NOW, Tomes was a fog-machined, spinning laser, Goth/Industrial fever dream. But half the walls in the main room dance floor were covered with book shelves full of volumes from floor to ceiling. The open walls between the bookstacks were simply black. Which, in and of itself, was strange, because it was too dark and hard to see—much less read—a book. And convulsing acid heads and leaping, raging drunks weren't looking for reading material. But I learned eventually that that was how the place got its name. I hadn't known a "tome" was actually another word for a book.

The music at Tomes was darker than the black walls and fitting except, again, we really didn't fit in. Especially me and Clarence. This wasn't tie-dyed Hippy Hollow or a rapidly, gentrifying upscale Austin. It was basically a back-alley, above-ground bunker for freaks and misfits.

It was always intense and we were typically surrounded by weirdos with black lipstick, black fingernails, black turtlenecks, black Doc Martin knee-high boots, black leather skirts, red and black pleated skirts, spiked dog collars (on boys and girls), mohawks, skinheads (of the non-Nazi variety), and more. God, I have to admit I had a thing for milky white, punk chicks with knee- to thigh-high black Docs back then.

The music was a DJ-ed cacophony of industrial, acid, goth and what people now call "darkwave" tunes, all accented by laser lights slicing through the smoky dance floor—all that in the primary front room, which was often half-empty. Or maybe it seemed half-empty because it was so dark. Regardless, we could always find our own table right off the dance floor. And, on the right kind of drunk, the laser-lit nightspot was almost hypnotic. But on a bad acid trip, I bet it seemed like an insane mash-up of A-ha's "Take On Me" video with films like *Tron* or *The Exorcist*.

Some of the music, some of the songs—I have to say "dark" was an understatement. Even after all these years, I remember some of the lyrics:

> *Last moment cries on the radio*
> *It's so hot down here*
> *Crushing metal bloody waters*
> *Same faces everywhere*
> *Now the anger is fading*
> *Now the fight can't go on*
> *We'll always be remembered*

Those lines were from "Don't Crash." I think it was by a band called 101. Or Front 242.

Actually, it was Front 242.

101 was a Belgian act and they had a song called "Rock to the Beat" (accompanied by a freakish claymation video with fish-headed dancers) that got regular play there. And I heard Bauhaus's "Bela Lugosi's Dead" every time I walked in the place. And Lords of Acid's "Sit on My Face." There was also always something by Ministry. Or Skinny Puppy. "Stigmata" or "The Killing Game." Sometimes "Every Day Is Halloween." And a song called "Warm Leatherette," which I often mixed up with "Don't Crash." I only knew the names because Hal did. He often played them on cassette tape mixes he kept in his car.

Some of the people who frequented Tomes were out there. Really out there. Figuratively speaking, it was a "nice" place to visit, but not the kind of place guys like me or Clarence wanted to live. Hal, either, I suspect. But he sure liked to wind things down there.

The back room of Tomes was something of a departure I think, but maybe not. A long bar for water or soft drinks was on the right when you walked in. And the walls on either side were completely different but also somehow entirely complimentary. As I think I said, we were always loaded, so my aesthetic appreciation and thematic interpretations may have been distorted.

If you were perched on a stool turned away from the back bar, taking it all in, the middle of the room was a dozen scattered, unmatching tables and chairs and a path to a small back patio. The haydite block wall on the right side was used as a large screen, which played F. W. Murnau's 1922 silent film, horror classic *Nosferatu* over and over on a loop. Every night. Which was creepy, but also kind of cool. I'd always been a horror fan. But the wall on the left featured portraits of baby heads, painted directly onto the wall. Sitting around in the back bar of Tomes was not unlike sleeping on Hal's black leather couch at the duplex. The babies' gazes followed you. There were at least two dozen, but they were not dead-eyed or grotesque a la *Trainspotting*. They were just babies.

Baby heads.

Baby faces.

Gerber babies on the left, *Nosferatu* on the right.

The back bar had more of a wind-down vibe, but it was dark and also usually seemed half-empty. There were always a few ecstasy-crashing Emos mesmerized by *Nosferatu*, and regulars murmuring or staring at nothing in particular in the corners. Hal was friends with a female bartender back there, and maybe a little more than friends. But if there was something going on, it was never in front of me or Clarence. They mostly just talked. If Hal wasn't a flailing, swinging, converted redneck dervish on the main dance floor, he was often talking to this girl.

She had raven-black hair, blue-green eyes and a sharp, aquiline nose. Of indeterminant ethnicity, she was built more like a slender Black girl than a White chick. And when she looked at you, she *really* looked at you. Even lit, it was somewhat off-putting. She had a weird flicker about her, but her eyes held you still. Hal chatted her up every time he went back there, and she seemed to get comfortable with him. I mean, female barkeeps are used to being hit on. But I'd occasionally see them together on the main dance floor, dodging the laser lights to their own separate, rhythmic cadences.

In fact, one of the few nights I remember driving home—in Hal's car, no less—we were bombed, but he wanted to stay out at Tomes. He tossed me his keys and said he'd take a taxi. I think Angela was with him, but maybe not. We'd all of us done things like that before: hang out a little longer, chase a girl, sap a buzz and then grab a cab. Or crash at somebody's place, sometimes with them in their bed. Sleep it off and have them take you home, or call one another and ask for a ride. I don't know if he went home with Angela or the Tomes bartender. But he came out of his bedroom around noon the next day and never mentioned it. He just walked in the living room in his boxers and stretched. "You up for some Short Stop?" he asked.

I was.

"Split Second"
Rigor Mortis

Short Stop Deluxe Burgers was a local burger chain that Clarence and I turned Hal onto. Now that I'm older I find it a little too greasy, and I'm trying to eat right or at least better. On some of those crazy nights (or early mornings) we hit Taco Cabana (which was open twenty-four hours) on the way back to the duplex or made a detour to the original Kerbey Lane Café, which is now a chain with a few locations. And one time Hal and I sat at the drive-thru line speaker of a Whataburger so long that neither of us heard the drive-thru cashier requesting our order. We had both passed out cold. Next thing we know, some poor, pimple-faced teenager was banging on the windshield. *"Sir, sir? Hello? Are you guys Ok?"*

The kid startled us awake and Hal peeled out and sped away without even ordering.

It was another preposterous instance of how we lived to tell the tale after some of the outrageous shit we pulled, stuff we should have gotten pinged for.

It was one of those savage Sixth Street nights— a Thursday I think—after a preliminary buzz at Dance Across Texas, a few buddy rounds at Maggie Maes or Toulouse (or both), a swirly two-to-three hours at Acropolis or Infinity, and then a wacked-out, black-light blowout at Tomes, that Hal disappeared. And not to a club across the street (which I forgot to mention he was wont to do) or a unisex bathroom stall with a one-timer or a *some-timer* (which he was also wont to do). He simply vanished in the billowy, laser-light sliced blackness of the dance floor at Tomes.

We thought he'd taken off with Angela or somebody else without telling us. Clarence and I took a taxi to the duplex, but Hal never returned. His car sat in a parking lot off Seventh Street until it was towed. Hal never came home and he never showed back up at work. He simply vanished.

The police asked us lots of questions at the time, but we didn't know anything. I think they also spoke to Angela, and she was pretty upset. The Austin PD eventually filed a missing persons bulletin, and Clarence and I talked to Hal's parents. We reached out to our mutual work and party friends and visited all the usual places. We did everything we could, but nothing came of any of it. Hal was simply gone. We got nowhere.

Clarence and I couldn't get our heads around it. Hal wasn't a flighty guy. I had known he backpacked through Europe one summer between semesters in college. And earlier that year he'd gone down to explore the Yucatán in Mexico by himself. But neither of those jaunts had been entirely unplanned. I couldn't see him running off without so much as a "Farewell," a nonchalant "Later" or a wink and a friendly "Fuck off."

And, besides, Hal's name was the only name on the duplex lease. But his parents let us finish it out. That was cool of them, but I think we all believed he'd show back up. I never even left the couch. I kept thinking Hal would walk out of his room again one morning in his boxers, or step though the front door sunburned and regale us with an epic tale about an ill-advised, but totally necessary month-long ramble in the Big Bend. Or months-long sabbatical in the Greek Islands. But it just never happened. The few times I ran into Angela after, she couldn't understand it, either. It was difficult to process. That time in Austin in the early to mid-90s—*Austin before the Austin it's become*—was one of the best times I ever had, and Hal was part of it. Mine and Clarence's lives went on, of course. But we never got any answers.

Sometimes, lately, though, I've dreamt about it. And even daydreamed about some of the crazy things we did. *Off the chain* or *next level* (in more contemporary vernacular) doesn't even begin to cover it.

"Warm Leatherette"
The Normal

When I got to the police station, things got weird and then, well, strange. Real strange.

I begged off work for an extended lunch break, still thinking the visit to the police station wouldn't take long. Detective so-and-so turned out to be Detective Grantham, a mid-thirtyish, ex-Marine-looking guy with a high-and-tight haircut and sports coat that fit a bit too snugly. I told Detective Grantham the same things I had told the police back then, and I knew I wasn't much help—but Grantham wasn't frustrated. He'd read the same stuff in the old reports. I suspected they had something new, and I sensed he wanted to talk to me about it. But he was very hesitant. He chatted me up some, but he was not exactly fishing. More like gauging. Maybe like trying to determine if I was rational, open-minded and reasonably intelligent. And it wasn't a condescending, racist thing—Grantham was white; it was more like an "are-you-prepared-to-hear-what-I'm-about-to-tell-you" type of thing. And I guess my response gave him a green light.

"You might be the only one who can help us on this, Evan," Grantham said. "This is a . . . this is a bizarre situation. Not like anything I've been involved in before. And we don't know what to make of it."

I was mildly stunned. But I nodded. "Yeah. Anything I can do. Henry was like a brother to me, really. One of my best friends, for sure."

"Okay," Grantham replied. And then another investigator, a lady, came into the room. She sat down next to Grantham and placed a manilla folder on the table.

"This is Sheila Drake," Grantham continued. "She's a Travis County cold case investigator who brought me in on this." Drake was also mid-thirtyish with bleached blonde hair, but conspicuously wore her police issue gun on her hip.

Drake smiled. "Hi," she said. "How are you?"

"Fine," I replied.

"You're not pressed for time, are you?"

"No, mam. Whatever I can do to help."

"You sure?"

"I'm sure."

"Ok," she replied, sounding as if I might regret it. "Here's the story. We've got a woman in custody. A young woman, actually. Says she's responsible for Henry Nilson's disappearance."

"How young?"

"Mid-twenties, maybe."

"That's not really possible. Hal—Henry—he disappeared twenty years ago."

"We realize that. We're aware of that. Not a clue or a lead in two decades. And in walks this lady . . . this girl."

"What—*is she his daughter?*"

"No. No. She's . . ."

"We have her confession," Grantham cut in. "She doesn't want a lawyer. She has refused legal counsel. She says she's guilty and she'll plead guilty. No muss, no fuss."

"This file isn't really a file," Drake added, referring to the manilla folder. "It's actually a confession. Her confession. That's why you're here. We . . . we'd like you to have a look at it."

"Why me?"

"Because maybe you can help us decide whether she's crazy or a frickin' time traveler," Grantham half-laughed. "The math is off. Her age—it's all obviously impossible. But the story she tells. It jibes with everything the department knew back then, and things you and Clarence said back then."

"She just walked right in and confessed," Drake said. "And then wrote her confession out. We were hoping you might be able to help us corroborate her story. Substantiate it. Or dismiss it."

"Did her confession mention me?"

"No. Not, specifically. Well, sort of. It mentions Henry. And it mentions two African American men he hung out with. It took her two hours. It's twenty pages long."

"Murderous"
Nitzer Ebb

They put me in a quiet room and I began reading the file. The confessor wrote it in the first-person. I recreated it here from what I remembered (and the poems and lyrics I looked up later online to be sure).

I worked in the rear area of an after-hours club called Tomes. Not after hours for me, really, but for the customers. Mere mortals, yes, but mortals who, like me, appreciated darkness. It wasn't a place people really went to pick up. It was a more like a haunt for the haunted. It was like a rave before the rave scene really caught on.

Henry was a little intoxicated the first time I met him, I knew. His speech was slightly slurred, but I didn't mind. He had bright eyes and broad shoulders.

The smaller, back bar I worked was lit mainly by Nosferatu, *an early 1920s horror film projected onto one wall. One night Henry sat on a stool at the bar serenading me with "Tainted Love," which was streaming in from the dance floor in the main room. But it wasn't Soft Cell's pop version. It was Coil's slow, black version. Devastating stuff. He could hardly keep the tune. But he was so intense. If you haven't seen the video, you should look it up. It conveys the real meaning of the song, the truth, the ugly truth all the "civilians" as Henry called them never realized or acknowledged. It was about the plague of the day. AIDS. I liked him immediately.*

I stopped reading and looked around. That sounded exactly like Hal.

I saw him about once a week for several weeks before we shared anything more than conversation. Intense conversation, which was refreshing. And songs. Sometimes he sang to me. Sometimes we sang together while I worked, him a lyric, then me a lyric. I remember it like it was yesterday. He loved "Over the Shoulder" by Ministry. And "So What." Have you ever really listened to "So

What"? Or read the lyrics? It was one of the few songs the DJs played the live version of at the club. I still know the words by heart. The whole song. They've never left me. They were prophetic, really. And the same is true of "Over the Shoulder"— We use them a while then it's over the shoulder—*like a discarded banana peel after we've consumed the fruit. Henry always said that's what people were doing to the entire planet. And he was right, of course. Look around.*

Our first night together was at my place. It was a modest efficiency in a small alley behind the Hyde Park Gym. The one that featured that giant, flexed bicep on Guadalupe. Like the club, it was full of books. Old habits die hard. Sure, the printing press was a welcome step up from quill and parchment. And reading under electric lights was an improvement over candles in most situations. But television never really did it for me.

Sometimes after we fucked, Hal would grab a book and started reading. Sometimes he read to me. Herman Hesse. Henry Miller. Poe. Translated Goethe or Nietzsche. Other times, I read to him, Baudelaire in French or Rainer Maria Rilke in German and then the translations. It practically brought him to tears. Do you know how rare that is in a mortal, especially now?

Sometimes Henry and I would fuck again and again and again. And after one particularly manic tryst, he rolled over on his back and started

How do they do it, the ones who make love
without love? Beautiful as dancers,
gliding over each other like ice-skaters
over the ice, fingers hooked
inside each other's bodies, faces
red as steak, wine, wet as the
children at birth . . .

. . . These are the true religious,
The purists the pros, the ones who will not
accept a false Messiah, love the
priest instead of the God. They do not
mistake the lover for their own pleasure,
they know they are like great runners:
they know they are alone
with the road surface, the cold, the wind,
the fit of their shoes, their over-all cardio-
vascular health—just factors, like the partner
in the bed, and not the truth, which is the
single body alone in the universe
against its own best time.

I, of course, purchased some copies of Sharon Olds' work and sprinkled them across the shelves at the club. Tiny traps for the unsuspecting. Truth as corruption—or liberation—depending on your experience or personal baggage.

I remember another occasion after a marathon romp when Henry and I laughed hysterically about a theological debate over whether or not Jesus Christ had shat. It was wrestled with by the great ninth-century theologian, Johannes Scotus Erigena. The pros were outnumbered by the cons, who argued that if Christ actually defecated, he couldn't be holy. Something along those lines. Henry had read about it in Milan Kundera's The Unbearable Lightness of Being. *I knew the story because I'd actually been in England around that time, and knew Erigena in passing—but I lied. I told Henry I was taking a break from pursuing a PhD in Medieval Philosophy.*

Henry believed me. Men always believe me.

The whole thing evolved into a hilarious discussion about coprophilia in Western literature. Henry talked about the pages Swift devoted to dispensing with Gulliver's excrement in Gulliver's Travels. *And I countered with Henry Miller's inimitable epiphany in the* Tropic of Cancer. *Something about what a miracle it would be if the miracle the faithful eternally attended to turned out to be nothing more*

42

I stopped reading again. Hal was a big Ministry fan. And I remembered that heavy version of "Tainted Love." But Hal never mentioned sleeping with this girl. The female bartender. Clarence and I suspected it, but we never knew for sure. The bitch sounded crazy, though.

I read on.

Sometimes we talked until dawn, and Henry held his own. Uncannily so for a mortal.

Henry knew things, and he shared things that . . . things that were disarming. One time while we were discussing the concept of Hell, a subject of which I am well-versed, he dismissed the supernatural aspects of it outright. "Hell is truth seen too late," he said.

And he kissed me.

He was quoting some British or American writer, I think. But still. Supernatural or not, it was true.

Truer than he even realized.

Fuck me, I thought, almost laughing out loud. That couldn't be a coincidence.

Sometime after I got back from my second harebrained stint at college, the owner of the market research firm decided to purchase a programmable, digital strip that ran messages from left to right across a screen all day. He had it mounted above all the cubicles on the main office wall, intending for it to be some kind of daily motivational tool. I think the owner actually believed that a daily dose of Zig Ziglar or fortune cookie clichés would somehow be inspiring to us. But, for some reason, they put Hal in charge of it.

Hardy-har-har.

It went okay at first. Hal dialed up pragmatic sages, like Ben Franklin for "A penny saved is a penny earned," stoic Virgil for "Fortune favors the bold," and even Nelson Mandela for "It always seems impossible until it's done." Cheery, positive stuff. Optimistic words in good, old-fashioned line with mom, apple pie and red-blooded American corporatism. But, after a while—I mean, he had to come up with something new every workday—Hal's quotes drifted. In fact, one in particular, led to his replacement as the firm's digital gladhander: *Hell is truth seen too late.*

Some of the God-botherers complained. And it probably happened around the time he was hanging out with the Tomes bartender.

I read on.

> *After that first night, Henry returned to the back bar at Tomes the following weekend. He didn't know I owned the club and, actually, the entire building. And the apartment strip where my efficiency was located. I didn't see any reason to tell him. Another night he asked me about the baby heads on the wall opposite* Nosferatu, *and I lied. I told him I didn't know why they were there.*
>
> *Henry played art critic and said the style of the brush strokes in every baby's head rendering was the same, and if you studied them intently, you might come to the conclusion that they all looked related. That, or the artist's range in terms of portraiture was limited. I didn't respond. I glanced them over myself and, surprised, silently agreed.*

If he only knew, *I thought.*

Henry was never anything other than intoxicated. If not by the alcohol or the physical urgency of dance, then by the hearts and minds laid bare in books. And by life itself. But he was also tormented by reality, the reality of life, of things. The reality of existence. There was a beautiful madness about him, something that was easy to pick out on a dance floor. He was all arms flailing, swinging, turning, jumping, sinking, rising . . . The dance floor was where he released his frustration and anger and despair. Mortal angst. But instead of being contemptuous of it, I was fascinated. He was enthralling. Some of you harbor an enchanting self-awareness and almost fairy tale-like wherewithal. But not many, even across the centuries.

I stopped reading again. Hal was my friend, and even though we'd only hung out together for a few years, he was like a brother. I was close to Hal in those days, but I didn't think of him in the ways she described him. Sure, he would get really real sometimes and say some heavy stuff. But the next minute we'd be laughing it off, talking shit. It occurs to me, now, that it filtered in and out, depending on the company, the context or his level of inebriation.

Sometimes we'd watch movies on the VCR. Usually, just stuff from the Blockbuster down the road. Hell, I was a *Godfather* guy, or *Heat* by Michal Mann. But we'd watch *Fast Times at*

Ridgemont High, Monty Python's *The Holy Grail* or even *Yellowbeard*. We'd already seen them a dozen times, and Hal would sit through them with us again. We enjoyed laughing it up together, hovered over Hamburger Helper or pizza deliveries (*We couldn't drink every night, for Chrissake!*) But Hal would also make the trek down to Vulcan Video to pick stuff up. We'd all already seen Spike Lee's *Malcom X* with Denzel Washington. But we'd never seen Denzel in *Cry Freedom*. Hell, *we didn't even know who Stephen Biko was!*

Hal would put on stuff we'd never heard of, like *Johnny Got His Gun*, *When You Coming Back, Red Ryder?*, or *The Crying Game*—stuff you never needed to watch again, because it left an impression. What do they say these days? *You couldn't unsee it.* To borrow an old song title from Public Enemy, Hal never really watched a lot of "Channel Zero." But that brings up another interesting point, now that I think about it.

We were listening to a lot of NWA back then, and bands like NWA and Ministry and Skinny Puppy had one major thing in common. They got zero radio time. They sold millions of albums through touring and word of mouth, but got zero radio play. Especially albums like NWA's "Straight Out of Compton" and Ministry's "The Land of Rape and Honey." This was before the internet and Spotify. There was a healthy underground music scene back then, and we were all inspired by it.

Anyway, Hal also picked up serious foreign films like *Wings of Desire* with that "Columbo" guy. Or *Zentropa*, with the creepy Max Von Sydow countdown at the end. And I remember a movie called *Mindwalk*, which Hal saw by himself at the Village Theater in Anderson Village before he knew me or Clarence, and then rented for us to watch later. Now, the Village Theater is an Alamo Drafthouse. But I remember *Mindwalk*, in particular, because it was exactly as billed. An intellectual stroll. A metaphysical meander. A little too arthouse, but still cool. Shit, the VCR was in the living room and I slept on the couch. Clarence could go on to bed in his own bedroom, but I basically had to watch this stuff or sleep through it. There wasn't a TV in every room like there is today. And I think, now, it was better that way.

This young woman who had confessed somehow knew Hal or she knew someone who knew him. Someone who must have seen him. Someone who also had to have engaged him, spoke to him. There was no other explanation. She might be crazy as a shithouse rat, but she knew some things about him.

It gave a me a sudden chill.

I dropped the confession on the table and stood up. Detective Grantham entered the room.

"Everything ok?" he asked.

"No," I said. "Not exactly. Who is this young lady? Where is this woman?"

"She's still in custody."

"Can I see her? From behind the glass or the mirror or whatever it is y'all do?"

"Why? Is her confession . . . are you saying that her confession is—"

"I'm not saying anything," I interrupted. "She just knows some things. She knows some things I don't know how she could know. And you're saying she's practically half my age. It's not possible."

"We didn't think so, either," Grantham continued. "I tried to brace her with that, but she's smart. She turned the tables on me."

"How?"

"She smiled. *She smiled*, almost as if for effect, and then put it on me. 'Jesus Christ died and returned from the dead over two thousand years ago,' she said. 'In your mind's eye, in your illustrations and films and paintings—does He even have a gray hair? Has He even aged a day? *Ha!* An hour? I know defying age is something we *girls* have to concern ourselves with more than you boys. But your *Savior* and I fell through the branches and limbs of the same family tree. His landing was just a little more graceful than mine. In fact, he's a Johnnie-come-lately compared to me. *Because I'm not descended from the Garden. I was there. And I came and went as I damn well pleased.* Why would you think I'd age any differently than Him?'"

"Wow," I said.

"Yeah, *wow*. Did you finish looking at the confession?"

"Not yet."

"Why don't you finish reading it? Do you need some coffee? Some water or a soda pop?"

"No. But what's going on here? This is crazy. Is it for real? Or are you guys trying to jam me up? I've been straight with you. I was straight with you back then. *I don't know anything new.*"

Detective Grantham shrugged. "We're not trying to jam you up, man. I told you, you're not a suspect. I think this young woman is trying to jam *us* up. I just don't know why."

Grantham turned to make his exit but stopped abruptly, and turned back around. "We believe you, okay," he continued. "But some things on our end have checked out already."

"Like what?"

"Did you get to the part about the state senator yet? The one she says she killed?"

"Yeah."

"His name was Cyril Thaddeus Randolph. He disappeared from the Driskill in 1932 and never turned back up."

"And This Is What the Devil Does"
My Life With The Thrill Kill Cult

I sat back down with the confession. I really didn't want to be there anymore. This girl was up to something or she was fucking crazy.

And yet.

I remembered flying down Mopac Expressway heading for Sixth Street (or Fifth or Seventh if it was the weekend—there was always more parking on Fifth or Seventh) and "So What" blaring in Hal's car speakers. *Who calls their band Ministry?* I don't think I could have made out what the Ministry guy was saying if Hal hadn't have been screaming along.

Scum-sucking depravity debauched
Anal fuckfest, thrill Olympics

Savage scourge supply and sanctify
So What? So What?

I loved Hal to death (pardon the pun), but maybe he had deeper issues than I realized. Or maybe I just wasn't very deep back then.

I went back to the confession.

> *Sometimes Henry showed up at the club with two black friends. Usually, a tall, skinny black guy with dark eyes, and the second a little shorter, more wiry. I think the taller one's name was Ethan.*

Shit, I thought. There it is. But there was no way. *Was this crazy girl the barkeeper's daughter?* I needed to get a look at her.

> *Sometimes Henry came with an attractive, young black woman. Sometimes he was alone.*
>
> *It never bothered me that he was fucking the black woman (I could smell her on him, and I knew there were others) because, early on, I only viewed Henry as little more than a good, intriguing fuck. Maybe a future kill. A meal for later. But that all changed. His intellect was surprising and his conscience bordered on terminal. He was aware of what was happening in the moment, even from the vantage point of his infinitesimally small mortal perspective in that moment. He was tormented by things that happened on the other side of the world. He talked*

about the ozone layer and the genocide in Rwanda. He stewed over man's inhumanity to man, humankind's suicidal extravagances and environmental abuses. It was almost shocking to me. How many mortals actually care?

Not even their god cares. Or he would have done something about it.

For most mortals, the endless hither and thither is their chief concern.

If I had ever possessed a particle of anything like maternal love or a penchant for compassion or nurturing in my long existence, I might have wrapped my arms around Henry and never let him go. I might have tried to shield him or protect him. He was doomed. His perception was too acute, and too conspicuous. His destiny would be a life of disappointment, alienation and perhaps even persecution. Men with torches outside his door. He was beautiful . . . and I don't mean that simply in aesthetic terms. I mean it in an existential sense. He was definitely too beautiful for this place.

That's why I'm here. That's why he was my last. June 1, 1994.

I stopped reading again. She even had the date right. But, like the year and place of a state senator's disappearance, she could have gotten that from a microfiche at the library with a few quarters.

But the rest.

I don't know if Hal was all she made him out to be. I don't think people think of themselves that way, and I'm sure he didn't. Yes, he read a lot, and even kept a decent-sized bookshelf in his bedroom. And he clipped strips of Matt Groening's *Life in Hell* (Groening's gig before *The Simpsons*—and edgier and more relevant than *The Simpsons* in some ways) out of the *Austin Chronicle*. And Michael Ventura's "Letters at 3 AM." But he also kept a few Joe Bob Briggs movie reviews. And he dug them just for the laughs.

Hal's intelligence was impressive, I admit. And one time I think I even asked him what he was doing there.

"Where?" he responded.

"Here? Austin? *Market research?*"

"Oh," he replied. "I told you. I'm taking a breather."

On another occasion, half-lit at a shot bar on Sixth Street, he mentioned he'd been awarded a graduate teaching assistantship and taught English comp to freshmen for a year during grad school. We may have been sitting across from some students from his alma mater.

"Yeah?" I egged him on. I thought he was just making a play for one of the girls.

"Yeah," he said, staring down a shot of Tequila. "It didn't work out."

"Why? What happened?"

He gulped the shot down almost absently. Everybody was waiting for him to answer, but I wasn't sure he would.

Finally, he did.

"The academy is a viper's nest," he said. "I ran my head, and they tried to lop it off."

I COVERED MY FACE with my hands and slid them up to scratch my head.

Jeez, I thought. What a fucking nightmare.

I slid my hands back down over my face and massaged my eyelids with my fingertips. Some lyrics ran through my mind.

> *I . . . just . . . don't wanna know . . . anymore*
> *Life shifts up and down . . .*
> *everybody knows it's wrong*
> *Life shifts up and down . . .*
> *everybody knows . . . it's wrong*
> *Why don't you care?*

"Smothered Hope," Skinny Puppy—with the lead singer of Ministry on vocals. Hal would be proud I remembered that. He knew every word to that one, too.

I flipped the page on the confession and kept going.

> *I knew what I had to do. You live for centuries and you kill out of spite or necessity. Human beings who are contemptible make it easy. Their agony and death are arguably even poetic. But I've heard mortals say things like "He ain't worth killing" or "A bullet's too good for him." A sense*

of loathing is something we all experience at one time or another. And justifications for killing, as well. It makes it all somehow easier for a mortal. They almost always concern themselves with moral considerations I dispensed with eons ago. And prattling on injudiciously about ending another being's existence is really bad form.

But I wondered if I had ever killed someone worth killing?

The notion vexed me. If you deserved to die, how were you not worth killing?

It was a strange axiom to me. But it led to my own epiphany.

It was so simple and yet so profound. I'd heard one of them say it a thousand times, but I never really listened. It was so cliché, I'd never thought of it in terms of meaning. Real meaning.

Being around Henry helped.

I realized later these clichés originated from concerns of possible ramifications or repercussions. The requisite societal consequences of getting caught. Being apprehended. Punishment. Life imprisonment. Execution. Perhaps even eternal damnation. But eternal damnation didn't apply to me. And mortality is a concern for mortals.

But whether or not someone was worth killing suddenly had meaning for me. I liked Henry. I actually looked forward to his company. I enjoyed him immensely—physically and mentally. But I soon realized what I'd discovered. What he actually meant—what Henry actually was. In *the scheme of things, I mean. And in terms of meaning.*

Henry was worth killing.

That.

That.

Yes. Henry was someone worth killing.

What could be more singularly evil of me, in a craft and passion where casual evil is a given? My kind can be as superficial and indeliberate as mortals. Henry was different, and taking his life would be different. I'm sure he was no saint, but I was accustomed to a steady, infrequent slaughter of misers, usurers, overseers, tyrants, misogynists, politicians, snake-oil peddlers and self-appointed prophets and profiteers of every stripe. The mischievous and the meek make human life Hellish already. Didn't killing them defeat the purpose?

Henry was an outlier.

Henry wasn't contemptible or meek. Henry was worth his next breath. Henry was worth killing.

We fucked again that night, with an intimacy that bordered on urgency. I knew it was me. How could something like me care about someone like him?

After we were both sated, I laid at his side, and then even placed my head on his chest. I could hear his heartbeat. "A single body alone in the universe against its own best time."

I almost fell asleep.

I realized I had to do it then, or I might never do it. I slid my tongue down his body and began licking his manhood, slowly, gently. I kept going until he was engorged. My eyes began to water.

As he reached climax, I used one forearm to hold his hips in place and my free hand to pin his neck to a pillow. I severed his erect member with my incisors, swallowing it in one gulp. He fought, but I was stronger. He gasped once, and I kept sucking. He struggled for a minute, but he was losing too much blood. Tears ran down my cheeks and I sobbed.

The sob shook me, but I kept exsanguinating him.

As Henry grew weak, I released his throat and he turned his head on the pillow. It was then that I caught sight of his face. Henry's head was lying on his left bicep and he was watching me. I almost stopped, but he didn't look hurt or even confused.

There may have been some horror in his eyes, but there was also something else.

His eyes. Henry's eyes. Did I mention they were green?

I took every last drop of his blood, and the green faded, his eyes left lifeless and gray.

It's almost silly and melodramatic to say—I do still read a lot—but it reminds me of the end of Fitzgerald's Great Gatsby. *The green light at the end of Daisy's dock, constantly receding. Except the green light is no longer receding. I extinguished it.*

Henry slipped away.

I took him from you.

I took him from you all.

I saved him from you all.

I paused, again.
Jesus, I thought. *Jesus.*

I consumed him. Marrow, flesh, all of him—except his skull. I kept it until I closed Tomes and decided to go overseas. I couldn't very well take his skull with me.

I had a country home a little farther north back then, and it was there. A few days before I disembarked, I stood with Henry's skull for a long time above the San Saba River. Several long moments. I . . . I'm getting over-literary here, but it was like the scene in Hamlet *. . . Henry as my* Yorick.

I dropped his skull into the water and just stood there.

I had consumed him and it was done.

It was done, but I felt different. Something seemed askew. I lost my appetite. I lost my joie de vivre, *if you prefer.*

Isn't that absurd?

Me, one of the furies, a demigod. It was exasperating.

I added one more baby's head to the wall at Tomes—the face of the cherub Henry and I might have produced had I not been a demon—and that was it. That was really it.

"Fuck that," I said out loud. *"Fuck that shit!"*

That's what those baby heads had been all along? *All that time?*

All that fucking time, that wall? It was a fucked up, fake maternity ward.

"My god."

Fucking insanity. I felt like spitting on the confession or ripping it to pieces. But I kept my cool. I kept going.

I left Tomes open for another year or two, and then closed it down. I sold the building. I traveled. I disappeared.

Florence, Madrid, Prague. Budapest. Istanbul. I had properties everywhere. But everything had changed. Something was different.

That's why I returned to Austin today. I came back to turn myself in.

I'll give you a name if you require it. I've had many. I even have social security numbers. But no authentic birth certificates or passports.

I murdered Henry Nilson in cold blood. Warm blood, actually. I ended his existence.

But how do mortals put it?

Ah, yes. The joke was on me.

Henry was a poison pill. I've been haunted by him ever since. Which I fully acknowledge the irony of. Killing human men is my nature. Why would I be haunted by following my own nature, fulfilling my own causa vivendi?

If nothing else, however, creatures like me are serpentine . . . and we can go long periods without feeding. I haven't had an appetite in decades. Not since Henry.

As I said. That is why I have returned. What's a 7,000-year-old sex demon to do?

What will become of me is hard to say. I reflect on it lately, more and more.

Is it possible for me to die? Am I capable of being executed?

Am I worth killing?

As far as what became of Henry, I can no longer escape it. He was my own true love. He was my dark heart.

I hereby confess to the first-degree murder of Henry Nilson on June 1, 1994. I do so of sound mind and form and freely submit my confession today, August 14, 2013. I do not want nor will I request or accept legal counsel. I am guilty and I'll plead guilty. My confession was not coerced or forced in any way. I record it of my own free will and of my own volition.

The signature at the bottom was hard to make out. It looked like she signed her name as "Lily Allatu."

I slid away from the table in my chair. Detective Grantham appeared momentarily.

I didn't say anything for a long time. I didn't know what to say. My first, unspoken, purely juvenile response was: *that crazy bitch bit his dick off!*

There was more to it than that, of course. Maybe she was sick in the head. Perhaps she was delusional. And that story about the baby heads.

Holy mother of fuck! We never went back to the rear bar at Tomes at night after Henry disappeared. But now, I obviously wished we had. I wished I had seen that last baby's face.

Would I have recognized it?

As crazy as the story was, however, it made me remember a lot about Hal, and think about it. And think about him with her. "So What" lyrics intruded in my brain, again.

> *My eyes, shit out lies*
> *I only kill to know about life.*

Fuck her. And fuck Ministry.

This Lily might be crazy and she might be full of shit. But she knew some things about my friend. You lose track of who you were and who your friends were. And what you were to each other. We romanticize some things and trivialize others. And sometimes the things we trivialized or downplayed were a bigger deal than we thought.

"What do you think?" Detective Grantham asked.

"I still don't know what to think," I admitted. "Like I said, she knew him or she knew someone who knew him. Fuck the math. She's describing Hal—Henry. She's describing a guy who was like a brother to me, but, in some ways, *shit*—in some ways, she seems to know him better than I did." I stood up and walked around the table. "I'll take that water, now," I continued, "but I'm sick of this. I'm sick of this bullshit. I want to see her. I wanna get a look at her. *Now.*"

Detective Grantham got me a bottle of water. I was thirsty and I drained it. Then, he led me down a hall to another room. We entered the room and it was dark, except for the wall that framed a two-way mirror. Drake's back was to us and the young woman was speaking to her. I had no experience with anything like it except seeing it on TV. I studied the young woman's face.

"Are you obtuse?" the young woman asked Drake. "You have your *man*. You have your *woe-man*. Do I have to explain it to you, again? Evil pricks are low-hanging fruit, dear. Men who make life Hell. Why settle for them? *Why let you all off the hook?* But Henry—Henry was neither evil prick nor low-hanging fruit. In fact, just the—"

When young woman stopped in mid-sentence, I could see her face in profile. I had that weird flashback, again. Hal was out on a dance floor full of freaks jumping up and bouncing around to a pounding techno/industrial beat, sliced by psychedelic lasers. Suddenly the music and the lasers stopped—and the contorting figures collapsed on the dance floor. And they lay perfectly still for several long beats in the dark, until the music and the lasers—dialed down to lucent scribbles—started again, really low. The dancers remained frozen. They didn't start moving again until the sounds were deafening and the lasers were a gamma brainwave. And then they were convulsive and spastic. Hal stood up and pulled this girl up with him—*Lily Allatu*—by her hand. And they smiled, swung away started bouncing around some more.

And the confessor slowly shifted her gaze to Drake and then over Drake's shoulder to the two-way mirror.

It was her, and she realized it was me. She knew I was there.

She looked right at me.

"Sensoria"
Cabaret Voltaire

Detective Grantham said I muttered something unintelligible and then fainted. He brought an EMT in immediately and they checked my vitals. Except for pissing my pants—which I hadn't done since I was eight or nine—I was fine. They let me come to on my own. I telephoned my boss at the newspaper and told her I wouldn't be back that day. And Grantham handed me a pair of fresh trousers from the police locker room.

"Do you think she killed Henry?" he asked.

I was shaky and played it off a little.

"She does," I said. "She seems too young to have done it to me, but she does look like the female bartender Henry hung out with."

They let me change pants and gave me a one-gallon Ziplock bag to place my soiled trousers in, and a tan paper grocery sack so I could avoid a walk of shame.

It had fucking been her, though, no question. Lily Allatu—or whatever the Hell her name was. She *had* been the female bartender Hal chatted up at Tomes in 1994 and she hadn't aged a fucking day. She was dressed more like Gwen Stephani or someone like that in 2013, but it was her. I was stupefied. And she could tell I was there. I think I fainted when she smiled at me. But I didn't want to sound crazy. And it wasn't my job to do their work for them.

Hell, she was doing that herself.

ALLATU STOOD BY her confession and they arrested her. The math was bad, but she knew some things she couldn't have known otherwise. They didn't have a body or any of Henry's remains, but they still indicted her. Her indictment made the papers, but never the front page. And never with any mentions or notes of paranormal or occult undertones. I sat for a deposition, provided testimony and followed the case.

Like the district attorney, Allatu fought the court's determination and subsequent ruling that she was criminally insane and not fit to stand trial. She was remanded to the custody of a fully accredited, maximum security psychiatric hospital in Vernon, Texas, and I went on with my life with my wife and kids. I shared the details with Clarence when he got back from overseas and we were both dumbstruck.

A few months later, I rang an old buddy named Carl, from Hal and I's market research days. He was a real estate guy, now, and I inquired about the building Tomes used to be housed in. I wondered if the wall was still there. I wanted to see it. I didn't mention it, but I wanted—*I wanted to see the baby heads*. Carl said it was vacant as far as he knew, but he would do some checking.

Carl got back to me the next day. He said it belonged to an old outfit called the Exodus Consortium. "Of course," I said, thinking out loud.

"You know them?" Carl asked.

"Not exactly, I said. But I heard something."

"What are you looking for?"

"Nothing in particular. I just wanted to see it."

"Well, an associate of mine still has a key. His firm represented Consortium for a while, but he said they never really tried to sell. They just shopped it a bit and then locked her down.

Locked her down.

The phrase froze me for a moment, like Allatu's tranquilizing gaze. "Could you get me in there?" I asked.

"Sure," Carl replied. "No problem."

CARL AND I MET IN FRONT of the old Tomes space a couple days later. It was locked up tight, and, besides the dust, fairly well preserved. The dance floor was still intact, and there were still some floor-to-ceiling book shelves full of volumes, some old, some newer. And flyers from the mid- to late 1990s. But the wall was gone. It had been replaced by load-bearing, Greek pillars. You'd never have known a wall had even been there if you hadn't seen it back then.

"You ever come to the bar that was here?" I asked. "Back in the day, I mean?"

Carl shook his head. "*Nahh, Ev.* This place was for freaks, man. Certifiable nutters."

It made me smile.

We explored a little and found a stack of really old magazines. The paper practically fell apart if you touched it. A *Harper's Weekly* from 1865 was open to a broadsheet turned on its side. "Holy shit!" I exclaimed.

"What?" Carl asked, a little startled. He came and looked over my shoulder.

The broadsheet turned sideways was a panel of illustrations from "Our Baby Show," drawings of babies after the Civil War.

Was that where Lilly got the idea? Was the baby head wall a record of confirmed kills? Or was there a tug in her she ignored or never admitted, even to herself?

Or, again, was she just fucking crazy?

"Shadowtime"
Siouxsie and the Banshees

Nine years later I saw her again.

This time with sky blue hair, but the same blue-green eyes. And it wasn't an accident.

I had had lunch with a colleague on Lamar. There are bistros over there now, and we had met at one of those. But on the way back to the office a young woman came toward me on the sidewalk with her eyes lowered. She appeared to be on her iphone and not paying attention to where she was going. But it was a ruse.

When the young woman reached me, she pocketed the phone and raised her head.

I started to say something, like *excuse me*, but she looked familiar. She immediately placed the tip and pad of her right index finger over the center of my upper and bottom lips.

I was startled and surprised. I recognized her, and my bowels quivered.

She still hadn't aged a day.

"It's okay, Evan," she said. "I'm not here to hurt you."

Her eyes held me still, really seeing me, same as back then. She nodded and I nodded back. She removed her finger from my lips.

"You read my confession?"

I nodded, again.

She looked away momentarily and seemed to shift her weight. Her profile was still striking. Shocking.

I still couldn't completely accept it, but there was no doubt in my mind. *She was the girl on the floor with Hal.* The girl he helped up. *She was the barkeeper.*

She held my gaze, again. "Do you remember that song, 'A Forest' by The Cure?"

"No," I answered. "I . . . That was more . . . They were one of Henry's bands."

"They were, yes. But all of ours, really, to varying degrees. There are a couple of lines. They're not in the original lyrics. I only heard the words at one of The Cure's live shows. Back then."

She paused, and then continued. "It was between the official lyrics and during the long instrumentals. In 1992, I think. Robert Smith sang *This kiss could cost my life, it's all you see in her eyes.*"

I took a deep breath.

"I only heard those lyrics at that live show," she continued. "But now I think about them all the time. I think about them and I think about Henry. And I wonder."

I exhaled. "You wonder what?"

"I wonder if . . ." she started, but seemed to reconsider. "There are not many mortals like Henry Nilson in this world," she continued. "He was my last. He will always be my last. Because he was the first."

"What does that mean?"

Lily smiled. "You knew him. He was a gift. And killing him was my gift—*and my curse.*"

She paused again, her eyes never leaving mine. "But now I wonder," she continued, looking away. She looked down and then refixed her gaze on mine. *"I wonder if he knew."*

It transpired very quickly.

I didn't understand everything she said, at first. But she disappeared as quickly as she had come. When I turned to watch her exit, she was gone. I didn't even call the police.

How did she get out of the psychiatric hospital? I vaguely assumed she might spend the rest of her days in a padded room as mute as Michael Myers.

But Michael Myers wasn't real.

Did they rehabilitate her? Did she get some kind of parole? Could someone or some *thing* like her *be* rehabilitated? *Or did what she did to Hal really make her quit cold turkey?*

I called Clarence and told him what she said. We were both flabbergasted and a little shaken.

HAL HADN'T BELIEVED in a Heaven or Hell, or an essence before we're born. He vehemently rejected the notion that there was a cupboard where souls are stored and dispensed in mortal coils by a higher power.

The older I get, the less I find myself in disagreement with him.

But how do I explain her?

How do I explain Lily Allatu?

Phantom Limb

Dr. Corbin got back to the El Capitan Hotel in Van Horn just in time for a quick dinner. The hotel restaurant was pricey, but the food was usually good. He ate alone at a table next to a window facing a pleasant courtyard and colorful fountain. It had been a long day.

Dr. Corbin got up early and drove south on US Hwy 90. The small community of Valentine was a blink; he didn't slow down until he reached the outskirts of Marfa. He spent the day milling around the overpriced galleries and a kitschy gift shop near the Hotel Paisano, and then detoured through Alpine on the way back.

It was just starting to get dark when he made it to his room at El Capitan. It wasn't much. Two queen beds and no couch, a small desk and a tiny bathroom right inside the door. When he entered the accommodation, he went straight to the bathroom without even flipping the overhead light switch on. When he came out of the bathroom, he was startled by something he hadn't noticed before. Actually, someone.

There was a man sitting in the shadows on the far bed. A large man.

"This is my room" was all Dr. Corbin could manage. Then, less than authoritatively: "What are you doing in here?"

The large man spoke. His voice was gravelly, and his accent was foreign. He spoke slowly and deliberately. "I was awaiting your return."

"Do I know you? I'm afraid I'm going to have to ask you to leave."

"Please refrain from doing so."

Dr. Corbin switched the overhead light on and immediately stepped back.

The man wasn't large. He was gigantic. His pale forehead was scarred and there was a chronic darkness around his eyes. His torso and shoulders, which seemed impossibly broad, were clothed in a dark turtleneck covered by a tattered wool sweater. Dr. Corbin was an average-sized man at best, and a pacifist to boot. He wondered if anyone would hear him if he screamed. "What can I do for you?" Corbin inquired, trying to remain calm. "I'm tired. I'd like you to leave."

"I shall. In due time. I would like to speak with you first, Dr. Corbin."

Dr. Corbin almost winced. "How do you know my name? I'm sure I'd remember you if we'd met."

"We are unacquainted, sir," the behemoth said. "And yet."

This is it, Dr. Corbin thought. I'm going to die in a West Texas hotel room. "This makes me very uncomfortable," he said.

"It should not. I just want to speak with you."

"What do you want to talk about?"

"Let us call it an itch, for now. I have an itch. It is a serious condition. I contracted it a long time ago. I cannot leave it alone."

"Have you tried Calamine lotion?"

The behemoth smiled. "It would not work."

"Why not?"

"It is not an itch on my skin, doctor. Or even in my skin."

"Where is it?"

"It is an interior condition," the huge figure replied, thumping his chest lightly with a fist the size of a small ham. Dr. Corbin took another step back. "Inside," the behemoth repeated. "Please sit down, sir. I have no intention of harming you."

"How can you expect me to believe that?"

"I should think that it might have been obvious. I could have destroyed you when you entered through the door. Or snatched you up with one hand and crushed you when you came out of the water closet. Or before we started this conversation. I could achieve it abruptly, even now. But, as I said, I have no intention of harming you. I bear you no ill will."

"Then what are you doing in my room?"

"I communicated that previously. I need to speak with you. About the itch."

"Why me?"

"You are a tenured philosophy professor at Texas Christian University. You earned a doctorate in Philosophy of Theological Studies from Boston University. I'm familiar with your work."

"How did you find me?"

"You are presenting a paper in Albuquerque in a few days. Driving in from Fort Worth. I assumed that Van Horn or El Paso would be the cutoff going. I wasn't sure where the return stop might occur. Also, your bio said you were an avid hiker. I know the Guadalupe Mountains have an excellent assortment of trails. And I knew Van Horn made the best base camp—with modern amenities—for accessing those trails. It was a good guess and involved luck. I thought I might accost you in the mountains, but the El Capitan seemed a reasonable place to start."

Dr. Corbin sat on his bed.

"The rooms are very small," the behemoth continued.

"Yes. They're pretty cozy, though. Especially for smaller . . .

"For smaller men."

"Yes."

"Small men go far in this life," the behemoth observed.

"Are you speaking literally or figuratively?"

"Both. Were you always diminutive?"

"I suppose I was."

"I never was. I entertain the possibility that being diminutive would have been enjoyable."

"You say you are familiar with my work. Have I written or said something that offends you?"

"No. Quite the contrary. You're just an academic, of course, but your erudition is serious. It has merit and enjoys some import."

"Thanks. Thank you."

"Thank you, sir. After all, it was I who sought you out. Are you more comfortable speaking with me now?"

"I suppose. What is your name?"

"Ah, yes. I call myself 'Adam.' It is something of a joke. I chose 'Inglok' for my surname."

"Scandinavian?"

"In the vicinity. But one more continent over, to the west. This continent. The term Inglok comes from the Inuktitut language, in the Great North, Canada, Alaska and Greenland. It is derived from the Inuit. An Eskimo term. Individually, they refer to themselves as Iñupiat —it literally means "real person." Many things you see on the ice in the Great North are not real. The Inuit called me *iglaak*. A traveler, a visitor. A stranger. I hail from Germany and migrated towards the pole when I was much younger. I call myself Adam Inglok. But I have no birth certificate or passport."

"Why's that?"

"I lived alone, near the pole, for many years. There were no close towns or carriages. Or railroads or cars. Just ice floe and the occasional Iñupiat."

"Why did you leave?"

"It began melting. And then the drilling started."

"Oil and gas?"

"Yes."

"They drill here, too."

"Yes, I am aware. But the landscape is hardly melting—it's simply being poisoned. And just as well."

Dr. Corbin shot the behemoth a glance.

"Apologies, doctor. That was my younger self speaking. The poisoning is terrible, of course. Reprehensible, to be sure."

"Yes. So back to your issue."

"Yes, yes," Adam said, thinking for a moment. "Can one experience an itch that is not there? Or in a part of them that, structurally speaking, may not exist?"

"I suppose so. Have you heard of a phantom limb?"

"No." The behemoth smiled. "Phantom limb."

"It's a sensation amputees experience. Sometimes, after they lose a limb—an arm or leg, for example, to military service, a car accident, whatever reason—they lose a limb and sometime after, even though they know the limb is gone, it starts to itch. Even after it's been removed. Even after it's no longer there."

"It still itches? They are actually compelled to scratch it?"

"Yes. It's fairly common."

"What do they do? How is the itch treated?"

"Therapy and physical rehab. They retrain muscles and joints. It eventually goes away."

"But a phantom limb, or an itch in a missing limb. I presume they must have felt the itch before. When the limb was still intact."

"I would assume so, yes. I think that's correct."

"What if they had never had the limb? What if they were born without it? Do you think they still might experience the itch?"

"That's a good question. It stands to reason that the answer might be 'no.' But I'm not sure there's ever been a study addressing the phenomenon or that particular circumstance. I'm sorry. And I'm not sure I understand. What is itching? Where are you compelled to scratch?"

"That remains the question, yes. I guess that's the . . . Do you believe in God?"

"That's not something I usually discuss, especially with strangers."

"I am simply an interested party, and it might be germane to our discussion. The devil is, as they say, in the details."

Dr. Corbin stared at the behemoth. "The philosophy of belief is my calling," Dr. Corbin said. "And it's not a position. It's a process. Sometimes I'm not sure I believe anything in a metaphysical sense. But I do have a belief system. If you're familiar with my work, you know this."

"Of course."

"I am less religious in a crowd. That may be why I come here once or twice a year. It's like you noted. I like to hike Guadalupe Peak when the weather gets cooler. It's the highest point in Texas. And sometimes when I stare out over everything from up high, I believe. It's humbling."

The behemoth was staring out the window again. "I explored the Swiss Alps once. When I was much younger. One might say a child."

"Really?"

"Yes. It was ages ago, now. I scaled Mont Blanc."

"I think you would find Guadalupe Peak tame compared to the Alps."

"Perhaps."

"I am fairly sure Mont Blanc is the highest mountain in the Alps and the highest in Europe west of the Caucasus peaks of Russia and Georgia. Just over 15,000 feet, I think."

"I did not know. It was a long time ago."

"Where have you been keeping?"

The behemoth continued to stare out a window next to the bed he was sitting on. "When I left the Great North, Greenland, I lived in Canada, Alaska and then Minnesota. Then, Utah and Colorado. Then, New Mexico. I prefer desolate spaces."

"So, when did you start experiencing this itch?"

"One hundred an—It seems like a hundred years ago. And it grows increasingly worse."

"Do you believe in God?"

"I do not know."

"Why did you ask me if I did?"

"It is a long story, but we will explore it, I think."

"The scar on your forehead. What's it from?"

"I hardly remember. It is from long ago."

"You skin looks dry. And pale. Does Texas weather agree with you?"

"I don't think so. But I shall grow accustomed if I remain."

"When do you experience the itch?

"It never leaves me."

"And you say it's an interior condition. A physical irritant? An inflammation?"

"No. Well, not entirely."

"If you want me to help you, you're going to have to be more specific."

"Yes. That is true. But I was hoping to establish a preliminary rapport with you, first. I don't want to frighten you."

"Frighten me? You frightened me earlier. I thought we were past that."

"We were. We are. But this is something different. Something unsettling, perhaps singularly unsettling."

"Do you really think you could scare me? On an intellectual level, I mean? You know my academic pedigree. You must realize that I've pondered Armageddon and Hell, studied them, lived with them for months and years at a time."

"Yes, of course. But, with all due respect, as scholarly subjects, abstract concepts."

"Perhaps. But do you honestly think you could say something frightening to me, something that I haven't heard or considered before?"

The behemoth smiled sardonically, but remained demure. "I fear as much, yes. I consider it entirely possible."

"Well, now I'm intrigued. I am not sure you're right."

"I am not convinced the specifics are necessary. This is the longest conversation I have held in a while, and I am enjoying talking to you. I don't want to . . ."

"Frighten me? Yes, I heard you. I've got to hear you out now."

"What if I think it unwise?"

"Humor me."

"Then answer my original question."

"What?"

"Do you believe in God? Or a god. Or even gods?"

"Why is that important? What bearing does it have on your condition?"

"Humor me."

"Touché, Adam. *Touché*. Hmmm. I'm not sure I believe in God with a capital 'G.' But I believe in a higher power. Something godlike, perhaps."

"A maker?"

"A creator."

"A divine creator?"

"A creator. A creative force."

"An omnipotent force? An omnipotent creator?"

"Something like that."

"Are you an essentialist?"

"Essentialist?"

"One who believes an essence precedes us, a spirit."

"A soul?"

"Yes."

"At some level, yes."

"You believe you have a soul?"

"That's not the term I would use, but yes. I believe—as you noted—we have an essence."

"All of us?"

"I think so."

"What about the animals? And the fish?"

"It gets complicated there, but, yes. I think so. A life force. The spark of life. What does this have to do with your itch?"

"We are arriving at that, I think. But I require further clarification, if you are willing."

"Sure. Okay."

"Dr. Corbin, you substitute 'spark of life' or 'life force' for the term 'soul.' Or 'spirit.' Do you believe all forms of life contain this spark or this 'spirit?'"

"Yes."

"What about inorganic life? No—wait. I refer, here, to life that is created unnaturally."

"Like In Vitro fertilization? Or artificial insemination?"

"Yes. Or utilizing fecundating semen from a sperm bank, perhaps from a dead soldier. The ejaculate is stored in small vials and cryogenically preserved in liquid nitrogen tanks."

"Couldn't it be argued that this process is part of a Creator's will? Or Creation's will?'

"Possibly. But life in either case is manmade. Does manmade life—does a manmade spark of life pass along a spirit? Is a spirit or soul . . . can a spirit or soul be introduced via unnatural fecundation?"

"Hmm, Adam. It's certainly a question worth asking. I don't think I could rule the possibility out."

"I do not think I can, either, within the framework of the discussion."

"What are your thoughts?"

The behemoth smiled again, but Dr. Corbin sensed a weariness.

"The Son of God was not conceived naturally," the behemoth said. "His conception is referred to as 'immaculate' because it was not the result of natural human coupling. Mary received In Vitro fertilization from God."

"That's an interesting way to put it."

"Would you phrase it differently?"

"I'm not sure."

"And yet, Jesus Christ is thought—believed— to have had a spirit, a soul . . . a Holy spirit, in fact. Perhaps the Holy Spirit incarnate. "

"Yes, but as you suggested, God was the In Vitro 'fecundator.' The standard precepts might not apply."

"I agree. But—Adam and Eve were arguably also created unnaturally, one from clay and one from a clay figure's ribs. Did they have souls? Would these exceptions not permit consideration of other deviations?"

"Another excellent question. In typical deliberations of other subjects, it would certainly give rise to special or separate precedents. It already has."

"We concur. And the next question involves cloning. And organisms created for tissue growth, but not sentient existence. Just development and harvest for foodstuff. Could either harbor a soul? Or a partial spirit?"

Dr. Corbin was stumped. "I don't . . . I can't imagine how." Dr. Corbin and Adam sat in silence for a long moment, the doctor pensive and Adam staring at the palms of his hands. The doctor eventually moved his pillows to the far side of his bed and repositioned himself so that he was sitting with his back to the headboard. "Adam," he continued. "You have obviously done considerable thinking on these subjects."

"I have had ample time. Eons, it seems. And, forgive the pun, but we are only scratching the surface." Adam clasped his hands together and, for the first time, Dr. Corbin noticed that one hand was discolored and maybe even larger than its counterpart. "It is true," the behemoth continued. "And it doesn't stop there. Increasing numbers of human beings are forgoing the grave or the crematorium and having their corpses placed in cryogenic stasis upon death. And this, after knowing full well that their spirit or their soul departs this physical realm and their mortal coil the moment they perish. Their rationale seems to be a desire to be reanimated at such time as medicine or medical technology advances to a point where the disease that terminated their physical existence or, in theory, death itself, can be cured or vanquished. But they are not asking an important question."

"It raises many questions."

"But the chief issue, I submit, is the one of soulless existence. Or, do you believe reanimation affords a second soul? Or that a soul never actually leaves the body? Or that a soul—like a corpse—can be reanimated?"

"Of course not. It certainly seems a quandary that requires . . . that demands, debate, exploration."

"We are in precise agreement on that, Dr. Corbin. But I might save the theorists some time and trouble."

"How is that?"

"That is what I have been scratching at. My scratching is metaphysical. My itch is metaphorical."

"I'm sorry. I'm not following you."

"Can I show you something?"

"Sure."

Adam leaned over, grabbed his turtleneck and the collar of his wool pullover with both of his massive hands and tugged them out and away from his neck. "Do you see that?" he asked. "Around my neck?"

Dr. Corbin leaned forward and stared. He sat back instantly and a chill ran down his spine.

There was a linear scar, with a track of rough stitching along the base of Adam's neck. And by the looks of it, it went all the way around his neck.

"What—what happened?"

Adam pulled his clothing farther away. "Look again."

Dr. Corbin glanced at the linear scar again and noticed slight discoloration in the skin around the stitching. Slight discoloration in the skins around the stitching. "That's not possible."

"No? What about this?" Adam's massive hands released his collar and lifted up his turtleneck and sweater from his waist. Pulling them up above his breast. His pale skin evidenced crude autopsy scars. Dr. Corbin stared in uneasy silence.

"Oh," Adam continued. "I saw you looking at my hands." He pulled the shirtsleeve of the larger hand up, just above the elbow. Another scar of rough stitching circumnavigated his wrist below the elbow. And the flesh below the elbow was slightly discolored, a different shade than the rest.

"How?"

"How?"

"Who are you?"

"You have not guessed?"

"No."

"Are you certain?"

Dr. Corbin didn't speak.

Adam continued. "Are you sure?"

Dr. Corbin trembled . . . "What are you doing?"

"Nothing. I need your help. I need you to help answer some questions."

"But, you're . . . What are you? Who are you? Are you a . . . ?"

"Am I a . . . ?"

"Are you a . . . a . . . victim . . . of some kind of medical experiment?"

"You might say that. Yes. It involved death."

"What? Are you saying . . . Do you think you're some sort of monster?"

Adam chortled with laughter. Dr. Corbin frowned.

Adam laughed again, and smiled. "Dr. Corbin, I am a monster, yes. But more to the point, I am the monster."

"That's ridiculous."

"Is it?"

"It's outrageous."

"Will you help me?"

"What could I possibly help you with?"

"You think me delusional?"

"I know you're delusional. Probably certifiable."

"Are you sure?"

"Yes. I'm sure."

"Would you like to be certain?"

"I am certain."

"As you wish. Will you help me?"

"Help you what?"

"The itch."

"The itch? Sure. Yes. Whatever. What itch?"

"The itch I cannot scratch."

"And what itch is that?"

"I do not think I possess a soul."

Dr. Corbin stopped and got quiet.

"I think I am missing a soul," Adam continued. "I think whoever I was before, some part of him . . . or them—they had souls. At some point in the past. A long time ago." Adam stared at his mismatched hands again. "But who I am now," he continued. "What I am now. I . . . I do not think I possess a soul."

"Why do you believe this?"

"Because of how I was . . . born."

"How were you—Nevermind."

"I am something of an amputee, myself, Dr. Corbin. But the amputations occurred postmortem. My father—he was driven. He wanted to defeat death. He wanted to destroy the manacles of mortality. My father stitched me together. And I was, how did I put it earlier? Reanimated."

"Reanimated. Right. And you think I would know or believe you? Why? Because I read Frankenstein in Ninth Grade AP English? Do you really expect me to believe this? Mont-fucking Blanc. That was a nice touch. Very clever."

"I am not concerned with belief. It does not matter in the least. I just want your opinion. It matters to—it is important to me. Will you listen and give me your opinion?"

"Sure."

"Thank you. If I was made the way I said I was made . . ."

"Yes?"

"If I was made the way I said I was made, would I harbor a soul? Would I have a spirit? That is the issue that plagues me. That is the conundrum I scratch at. I rake the surface to see inside. To understand fully. To know with certainty. Am I damned? Was I damned at birth? Or rebirth, as it were?"

"This is . . . This is silly. Do you expect me . . . Do you?"

Adam leaned in and smiled grimly. Dr. Corbin got the closest look at the behemoth he had had all night. Up close, Adam's eyes seemed mismatched, but they bore a dull light. He carried the scent of road kill, something dead and drying up. It was jarring. Corbin recoiled and almost shat himself. And he remained at an arm's length—a mortal's arm's length, anyway—away from Adam.

The behemoth leaned back, finally. "I am a creature of blunt force. I have never felt the caress of God. Or a god. I have no sense of an innate force or spirit guiding me or comforting me. Or the notion that I might be nourishing a force or spirit with my behavior or general proclivities. I thought I would expire up there, in the Great North. I thought I would die and my remains would drift out into the black seas. That my spirit, if I possessed one, would finally be at peace. But I did not die. It seemed I could not die.

"Mary Wollstonecraft Shelley's book was fair, if not completely accurate. And it concluded the way I thought I might. I left my father dead on a frigate and went to build a funeral pyre. I snuck back to the vessel after midnight and stole a wooden lifeboat and a torch and gathered what spare wood and flotsam I could besides. I crushed the skiff and I constructed a pyre and set it aflame. I waited until the fire was hot and the flames were high and stepped aloft, prepared to die. The flames rose farther still and I thought I might see my end, but the ice under the pyre was shallow. The piping hot coals and the flames melted the icy floor and the conflagration and I fell through. I drifted under the ice and then reemerged farther out.

"That was two centuries ago, now. I wandered the Great North. I studied the Inupiak and the polar
bear and the wolf. I sank into the depths with the whales. I subsisted on seal, caribou and muskox. And seabirds and their eggs. And cod and char. Where children's daydreams conjured up Santa's Workshop or your Superman's 'Fortress of Solitude,' there was only me, a wandering wretch. A monster. The monster. Adam Inglok. Deformed within and without.

"It hasn't been a bad life, but I am aged finally, and incrementally, decrepit. And I suffer from a metaphorical itch.

"I was the death of my father, Dr. Corbin, who, in truth, was also my mother and my creator. He gave me life, presumably without divine spark. And I murdered his wife and son. I suspect I do not possess a soul. If I have a soul, I am not sure I would be welcome in heaven. But even in hell, I would no longer be alone. If I have no soul, will I be welcome in either? Or will I simply perish and my consciousness end?

"That would not be entirely disagreeable," the behemoth continued. "But I would like to know, Dr. Corbin, sir. Do I enjoy animus in a traditional sense, or am I simply fleshy Golem? The question is the only suspense I enjoy as my story comes to an end."

The tormented behemoth slid off the bed and rose to his full height. Dr. Corbin felt his stomach drop.

"Dr. Corbin, sir" the behemoth said. "Do I have a soul? Is there an afterlife for an afterlife creation? Is there an afterlife for a man without a soul?"

Dr. Corbin remained silent. He didn't know what to say.

The behemoth stood waiting.

"Where will you go?" Dr. Corbin inquired, finally.

"I am unsure," the behemoth said. "The Gulf of Mexico, perhaps."

"I'm sorry for . . ." Dr. Corbin began. "I'm sorry I couldn't . . . I'm sorry, Adam. I truly am."

"I am sorry, as well," the behemoth said, smiling grimly. "Thank you, sir, for speaking with me."

Adam crossed the room in two steps and opened the door.

He left without looking back.

Sad Potatoes

Ben watched sadly.

In his simple mind, this was the saddest funeral he had ever seen.

An old woman wheezed and moaned. A taller, middle-aged man sniffed and sobbed. The preacher's soothing voice seemed to somehow exacerbate their grief, and Ben wanted him to stop; but all he could do was cry.

So sad, he thought. So much hurt.

Ben had been to seven funerals in the last three months, and each one saddened him more.

At first, he was only slightly sad because he was mostly mortified. The ritual was frightening and freakish to him. At his second funeral one of the mourners had propelled herself onto the deceased's coffin as it was being lowered and screamed "Take me, Lord! Oh please, Lord. . . take me instead of him."

The spectacle had terrified Ben. He wrapped his arms around his head and cried out.

The other mourners had simply panicked, not knowing whether to dislodge the leaping, begging woman or console the screaming half-wit. The last few funerals had been mostly uneventful. Ben had been mostly just sad.

Sometimes when Ben was sad at a funeral service, one of the older, blue-haired ladies would pat his shoulder to comfort him, or look up at him and say things like "There, there, young man. It's okay. He's gone on to a better place . . . we should only envy him."

Ben would nod and swallow, wiping his tears with his shirtsleeve.

Ben knew they were right. His Aunt Ruby had told him so.

Before every meal and bedtime, Ben and Aunt Ruby thanked the Lord for His blessings and prayed for forgiveness and salvation. Aunt Ruby constantly impressed upon Ben the importance of the Lord in their lives, and Ben often felt blessed and forgiven and saved. Though we wasn't sure what he needed to be forgiven for or saved from.

Ben prayed for preachers and worshippers and neighbors and Aunt Ruby and all the kids he could remember on the milk cartons. Sometimes he even prayed for his dead dog, Larry, and his parents, even though he knew that they, too, had gone on to a better place. Aunt Ruby's heart was filled with warmth-eternal when she watched her huge nephew kneel next to his bed and pray like a child.

"Blessed are the meek," she would whisper, when she crept by later to check on him.

Ben's funerals came in the afternoons after working in Aunt Ruby's garden. His devotion kept it a formidable county landmark.

Encompassing most of Aunt Ruby's back yard, the garden yielded some of the area's largest melons and cucumbers, and the county's sweetest potatoes. Ben was the first to till every spring, and only the Sabbath kept him from weeding and raking and watering. He carefully concocted every compost and meticulously attended to every stalk and sprout.

Ben's potato crop was his pride and joy; Aunt Ruby's soil was made for his spud slivers and every tuber section—placed six to eight inches deep and spaced fourteen to eighteen inches apart—sprouted in no less than two weeks, and every eye produced at least a half-dozen Bliss Triumphs, the state's native spud. Even when Ben's Bliss Triumphs went head-to-head with Irish Cobblers and Idaho Russets, he still brought home blue ribbons for the county's biggest tubers.

When it became too hot to work in Aunt Ruby's garden, Ben would usually clean up and have lunch. Sometimes he went to town to browse through the local hardware shop.

Ben loved the Ace Hardware shop and he kept a clipping of the latest John Deere 42-inch Hydraulic Tiller in his wallet. It had a reversible till design that allowed for forward and backward tilling, and he enjoyed sitting on the store model and imagining himself plowing through monster pigweeds, rabid dog fennels and threatening buckthorns.

Lately, however, Ben had been spending his afternoons at the town cemetery. He discovered it one day after following a slow, winding procession of cars and trucks into the pasture the cemetery occupied. The crowd had piqued Ben's interest and he had followed them. And being part of the procession had made Ben feel somehow important.

After lunch, Ben often cleaned up, put on his church clothes and headed to the cemetery. When Aunt Ruby asked him where he was going, he would smile and say "Allison Rest." Aunt Ruby knew he meant the Elysian Rest Cemetery and she would always remind him to avoid strangers and stay off the road. "Remember what happened to Larry," Aunt Ruby added.

But Ben could never remember what happened to Larry.

The first time he tried to recall what happened to Larry, he had nightmares for a week. He envisioned the bloody, white, passenger-side quarter-panel of a 1977 AMC Pacer. It was sort of like the "white-light-at-the-end-of-the-tunnel" dream that Aunt Ruby and her friends occasionally discussed at the Quilt Club gatherings that she held in their den the second Tuesday of every month. Except when Ben got to the end of the tunnel—which invariably smelled like mulch and the Sulphur stuff he sprinkled on the squash to protect it—the bright light was really the blood-smudged, white quarter-panel of the Pacer. It scared him and made him sad. He didn't understand.

The walk to the cemetery was short, but it gave Ben plenty of time to think about things like Aunt Ruby's garden, the quarter-panel and the suffering he witnessed. Even in his simple mind there was a haunting sense of wrongness about the hurt and a desire to fix it, and on the afternoon of the saddest funeral he had ever seen, something clicked.

"Harvey was a good man," the preacher said, in his soothing tone, the drone of his voice floating off as surely as Harvey's soul. This particular preacher was Ben's favorite. He was always dressed in black with his hair combed back, perpetually solemn and serious; and he always concluded the service with personal remarks, anecdotes—stories that repeatedly made Ben wish he was the man or woman being lowered in the coffin, the lucky one, on his or her way to a better place.

"Harvey was a good man," the preacher repeated, as if remembering. "He's left us for now, but he's gone on to a better place." And in Ben's mind—at first murky and undiscernible, but suddenly perfectly clear—it finally made sense.

As Ben stood there behind the wheezing old lady and the tall, sniffing man, looking over their shoulders at the preacher and the open grave, he had a revelation, just like the ones Aunt Ruby read him from the Bible.

Ben thought of the hereafter. He imagined Heavenly fields, all green and flourishing. He saw all the happy souls arranged in row after row, acre after acre (like his Bliss Triumphs), and it all came together. All the unhappy, weeping mourners were sad because they had been left behind. All the poor old people and pitiful young people were hurting because their friends and loved ones had gone on without them.

Ben finally understood, although it was a comprehension he would never be able to put into words. He knew what the Bible said about man being made from the dust of the ground; and he knew from the garden that a seed had to be planted in the ground before it could grow. As Ben stared at Harvey's coffin and surveyed the grave that it would soon be placed in, he had an epiphany. He knew what he had to do. He wiped his eyes and slowly stepped forward.

He was smiling tearfully, compassionately, when he seized the old woman and middle-aged man in mid-whimper and brought their heads together with a loud "Thwack."

They fell away like discarded marionettes, their surprised glares seeming to confirm Ben's notion. He smiled wider and held his arms out to the preacher.

The preacher's soothing drone broke when he recognized the approaching hulk to be the screaming half-wit from the frightful memorial where the hysterical widow had launched herself onto her husband's coffin. As if that wasn't nightmare enough, he thought, and then trembled.

Ben only beamed.

Ben's favorite preacher slowly began backing away as he approached and, for a moment, Ben thought the preacher seemed unsure about his own deliverance to the sweet by-and-by. But the preacher quickly regained his composure and started to

speak. As Ben wholly embraced him, the preacher attempted to say "My son," but he never got past a hiss of the "S" and his cracking spine and death rattle were accompanied by a shrill, long "A" groan and a guttural slur.

After a moment, Ben released the preacher from his embrace, but took the lucky man's face in his large hands and kissed it. There was only love in his deliverance, and he was well-pleased that the preacher seemed to recognize him for what he was as his back snapped.

A savior.

TO KEEP THE SUN from parching his new strain of Bliss Triumphs, Ben peeled away their sackcloth and moved them into the nearest shade. After a quick trip home to change back into his work clothes, he returned to the cemetery with his tools.

Ben spent the rest of the afternoon preparing slivers and readying the new garden to receive them. People's eyes were bigger than a potato's and, after an early afternoon breeze came he carefully began planting them six feet deep and fourteen to eighteen feet apart. He finished just after dark.

On the way home Ben wondered at the pain he would be able to alleviate and all the hurting he would now be able to cure. And he felt a grown-up sense of satisfaction—maybe for the first time ever.

He knew working two gardens would be hard. But he was inspired.

Definitive Act

Eladio had scoped the mailbox out for three days. It was on the edge of the barrio in the vicinity of several boarded-up businesses. There wasn't much traffic and there were no working pay phones anywhere close. He worried about being seen, falling into the street or somehow making it to a working pay phone.

This would Eladio's *acto definitivo*. For as long as he could remember he had dreamed of doing something remarkable, something that when people studied the map of his shitty life, they would point to this moment and say that this was who Eladio Segura was. Not the drugs or the gang stuff or the trouble that always seemed to follow him around. He would redraw the lines of his existence. People would know who he really was. The beginning and the middle wouldn't matter. Only the end.

Eladio was certain that the police would think his death was just another instance of senseless street violence. That he was just another *pendejo del barrio* dead at the scene. He was also pretty sure his Abuela might get microphones stuck in her face for comment, and he felt bad about that. But he knew what her answer would be. She would be on TV saying her grandson had never had an enemy in the world.

It didn't matter.

By the time they figured out what had happened, it would be too late. But it would also be okay, too.

ELADIO PLACED A 12X9" manilla envelope on the top of the faded blue, graffiti-pocked USPS mailbox around 1:30 in the afternoon. He had skipped breakfast, school and lunch. He'd heard too many stories about people shitting their pants when they died. He didn't like it, and, even as ridiculous as it sounded, he felt it was unbecoming of *un acto definitivo.*

The envelope was not the normal kind. When he bought it, he made sure it was self-adhesive because he wouldn't be able to lick it. He thought about rereading the note, but he'd poured over it for hours and reread it a dozen times. It said what it needed to say.

Eladio pulled a red bandana out of his back pocket and wrapped it around his upper left bicep. He looped a granny knot in the bandanna, and pulled it as tight as he could using his front teeth and his free right hand. Then he pulled a new razor out of his shirt pocket and removed the protective cardboard sheath that covered the blade.

Eladio knew he would have to move fast. Even with the bandana around his arm, he would bleed like a stuck pig . . . and that might give him away. His only other concern was the letter getting caught at the post office. But the manilla envelope was thick-stock and he had inserted a piece of thin cardboard that he removed from the back of his sketch pad. He was sure the letter would make it through. It had to.

He removed the adhesive strip from the envelope but left it open. He placed the razor between the thumb and index finger of his right hand and then surveyed his surroundings. There was no one in sight.

He turned his left wrist up and held it out and away from his body. He dug the razor blade into the left side of his wrist where it met his hand and slashed inward and diagonally across. Blood jutted from the slit.

Still holding the wound away from his body and the mailbox, he loosened the hand-made tourniquet and draped it over the wound. Then, he placed the razor blade in the envelope and sealed it with his right hand. He dropped it through the drop slot and began walking away. He held the bandana in place with his right hand. He didn't want to lose too much blood near the mailbox.

After Eladio had walked a half-block, he removed the bandana and let his wrist bleed freely. The blood still came in small spurts.

When he knelt down to drop the bloody bandana into a gutter slot, he almost fell over. He was scared for a moment, but he had known he would be. He had planned well. No close pay phones was a great idea—but not because he was changing his mind.

It wasn't so bad. And he was going to pull it off.

The Rio Grande Valley sun suddenly seemed hotter, and he felt a little dizzy. His mouth was dry and his whole body seemed to droop, but he wanted to remain lucid. He started to jog. His stride was drunken and he stumbled, barely recovering. He thought about his girlfriend, Julie. He knew his letter would make it. He began to cry, but he was not afraid.

Eladio's blood was barely dribbling from his wound now, and his skin was turning gray. His moment was gone.

The sun seemed less oppressive and he grew cold. He collapsed to his knees and fell forward. His head came to rest on a patch of dingy grass just off the cracked sidewalk. He turned his face toward the mailbox. No one was near it.

His breath was short. His shallow puffs shook the grass near his lips. He didn't have much time. His muscles seemed to leaden, but he turned his head to face the sun. He stared at it for as long as he could.

His eyes never closed.

ELADIO WAS RIGHT. And lucky.

A short spring rain came later that afternoon, washing away some of his blood. And the police ruled his death a homicide. They said there appeared to have been a struggle and Eladio, wounded, had fled. And though they had no suspects and hadn't found a murder weapon, the investigation was ongoing. One of the police detectives recognized Eladio and said he wasn't surprised.

Eladio's friends and classmates were stunned. A few were quick to tell reporters that Eladio had really seemed to be turning things around. When the news got to Julie at school, she ran into a bathroom and threw up. Then, she refused to come out of the bathroom stall.

Julie hadn't heard from Eladio in a few days. Her father had threatened Eladio and ran him off. She had pled with her father and begged him to reconsider, but he wouldn't be swayed. The thought of his daughter going with a "wetback" (as he called Eladio) and a troublemaking wetback at that, made his stomach sink. He decided that Julie would simply have to move on.

Julie hovered over the toilet sobbing lightly. Her friends took turns trying to coax her out, but she refused to respond.

IT TOOK THREE DAYS for Eladio's letter to make it through the postal system. It did so undetected.

The letter arrived at Julie's house just after Eladio's funeral. Julie's mother and father had attended the service, and her father—even as much as he disliked Eladio—felt bad about the boy's death and tried his best to support his daughter. It was easier to support her with Eladio gone.

The funeral was a large, outdoor affair with half the high school in attendance. This surprised Julie's father, but he didn't let on. Father Gonzalez from the historic Immaculate Conception Cathedral said a few words about tragedy and forgiveness and salvation, but kept things brief. It was hot and there was very little shade. The Rio Grande Valley sun bore down on the funeral service as if through a magnifying glass.

Tears streamed down Julie's cheeks, but she kept her composure. Her father was surprised by the depth of her grief. In a brief moment of panic, it occurred to him that Eladio might have taken his daughter's innocence, but he refused to accept this possibility. And if he was wrong, he didn't want to know. Still, he took one of her hands and squeezed it, expecting to get her attention.

Julie didn't acknowledge him, and he released her hand.

Eladio's abbreviated family was situated almost opposite of Julie's through the entire ceremony. They seemed more irritated than agonizing, and ignored Julie entirely. She wondered if Eladio had encountered resistance to their relationship as well.

Eladio's grandmother's eyes were sad but dark and stern, like his. Julie couldn't help but stare at her, but never for very long. She was afraid Eladio's grandmother would catch her.

Eladio's grandmother wept quietly, gently dabbing her eyes with a white handkerchief and occasionally shaking her head and peering up into the sky.

After the funeral, Julie and her parents returned home in silence. Julie's dad had decided that the best way to respect her grief would be not to be a hypocrite. He despised hypocrites more than anything else. He wouldn't speak of Eladio unless Julie initiated it. And he hoped she wouldn't.

Julie's brother had skipped the funeral and arrived home from school before the rest of the family. He got the mail and placed Julie's new *Miss* magazine and a manilla envelope on her bed.

When Julie got to her room, she pushed the magazine and the envelope to the side of her bed and laid face down in her pillow. She closed her eyes and began to cry. Her mother heard her muted whimpers and closed her daughter's door.

Eladio had made Julie feel special. Eladio had made her feel like a better person than she knew she was. When someone thinks of you in that way, you try to live up to it. You try to be that person. You want to be better—and she wanted to be better. She and Eladio talked about all the things they would do, where they would go. Eladio made her feel perfect, and her dad ran him off. Her father made a choice for her, and now the one person who made her feel really special was dead.

After a while, Julie rolled over and opened her eyes. Her cheeks were red and wet with tears. She felt the magazine under her elbow and retrieved it. Once she discovered what it was, she flung it across the room. She grabbed the envelope and held it up. No return address. It looked like junk mail. She started to throw it as well, but dropped it on her chest instead. She wiped her tears and tried to compose herself.

She picked the manilla envelope back up and opened it. She examined the thin cardboard stock inside and noticed a speck of deep scarlet, almost black. There was a letter written on notebook paper. She removed it and gasped. She recognized Eladio's handwriting immediately. She sat up and tears began streaming down her cheeks again.

Julie read Eladio's letter in shocked silence. She noticed dried specks of blood in the upper righthand corner. She began crying again and didn't stop for a long time. When she did her lips still quivered, but she managed a strange smile.

Julie read the letter again and again and then held it over her face. Her tears made the ink run. She would never let another boy talk to her the way Eladio had. And she would never talk to another boy the way she talked to Eladio.

Julie turned the envelope upside down and the razor dropped into her lap. It had a trace of rust and dried blood on it. She held it flat against her cheek. Then, holding the blade side between her fingers, she slid the blunt side down her cheek to her neck and across a jugular vein. Fresh tears came again.

The razor felt warm.

WHEN JULIE ENTERED the living room her dad was sitting is his recliner watching cable news and her mother was reading a book on the couch. Neither looked up.

If they had, they would have noticed the bloody footprints that trailed Julie on their light-colored, Berber carpet.

Julie had the blood-soaked manilla envelope in her left hand and she was carrying it by the envelope flap.

By the time her dad looked up, she was standing over him. Her face was flushed and blood was running down her chin. Her cheeks were puffed out like a chipmunk's and the front

of the dress she'd worn to the funeral was covered in blood.

"Julie!" he cried. *"What happened? What's wrong?"*

Julie's mother looked up and began screaming.

Julie tipped the blood-soaked manilla envelope upside down and dumped her tongue into her father's lap.

He squirmed away from it and fell out of his recliner. Her mother stood up, still screaming, and tried to help him.

Julie smiled.

When the blood that filled her cheeks drained out of her smile, you could almost see the whites of her teeth.

TYTUS BERRY is the *nom de plume* of an author who resides off the grid in far West Texas. His first piece of horror fiction, "Phantom Limb," was published in the Lone Star state's annual horror anthology, *Road Kill: Texas Horror by Texas Writers*. When Berry isn't travelling back roads, forgotten roads or plain old dead ends, he haunts state and national parks in the region.

P.O. Box 10533, River Oaks, Texas 76114